SEARCHING FOR SASQUATCH

NATHANIEL LACHENMEYER

ILLUSTRATED BY VICKI BRADLEY

SASQUATCH BOOKS
SEATTLE

For the Rabbit King

Text copyright ©2006 by Nathaniel Lachenmeyer
Illustrations copyright ©2006 by Vicki Bradley

Printed in China
Published by Sasquatch Books
Distributed by Publishers Group West
15 14 13 12 11 10 09 08 07   9 8 7 6 5 4 3 2 1

Book design by Bob Suh

Library of Congress Cataloging-in-Publication
Data is available.

ISBN: 1-57061-442-3

More about the author at www.NathanielLachenmeyer.com.

119 South Main Street, Suite 400 • Seattle, WA 98104 • (206) 467-4300 • www.sasquatchbooks.com • custserv@sasquatchbooks.com

AUTHOR'S NOTE

Sasquatch is a Native American word that means *Wild Man*. Most people who have seen Sasquatch agree that it is very large and that it looks a little bit like a person and a little bit like a gorilla. Not many people have seen Sasquatch—not enough people have seen it for everyone to agree that it really exists. Some people think that Sasquatch lives deep in the woods and hides from people. Others think that Sasquatch exists only in our imagination.

Arlo and his father had never seen Sasquatch,
but they believed that it was out there,
waiting to be discovered.

Their favorite thing to do was hike through the woods together, searching for Sasquatch. Sometimes, they saw bears. Sometimes, they heard a moose call or caught a glimpse through the trees of a bald eagle flying overhead. Once they even saw a wolverine.

Arlo's father knew all about the animals and plants
that lived in the woods, and he taught Arlo everything he knew.

Arlo marked down on their map where they hiked and took photographs of everything they saw. They didn't find Sasquatch. But it didn't matter. They both loved adventures, and there is no better adventure than searching for something that is hard to find.

On the first day of school, Arlo's teacher asked the class what they did that summer. When it was his turn, Arlo told everyone about his adventures with his father.

After Arlo sat down, his teacher
turned to the class and said,
"There is no such thing as Sasquatch.
Sasquatch is just a myth."

When the bell rang for recess, the biggest bully in Arlo's class and his two best bully friends marched through the halls, shouting that they were Sasquatches. For the first time, Arlo felt ashamed of his adventures with his father.

Arlo went hiking with his father that weekend. But he kept thinking about what his teacher had said. Suddenly, he noticed something in the dirt: the largest footprints he had ever seen. "Dad, look!" he shouted. When his father saw the prints, he gave him a big hug and smiled. "Those are definitely Sasquatch footprints," he said.

Arlo took photographs of the footprints from every possible angle. He couldn't wait to tell everyone at school what they had found. This was a major scientific discovery!

The next morning Arlo told the class about his discovery. The bully pulled two Sasquatch-sized wooden feet out of his knapsack, and asked, "Did the footprints look like this?"

That evening at dinner Arlo announced
that he didn't believe in Sasquatch anymore.
When his parents asked him why,
he showed them the wooden feet.

Arlo expected his father to say that he didn't believe in Sasquatch anymore either. But he didn't. Instead, he looked at the feet and said, "Let's try them out."

Arlo's dog, Stanley, followed them to the front yard and watched as they pressed the wooden feet into a patch of soft earth.

Arlo's father examined the footprints. The prints were identical to the ones they had found in the woods. He smiled. "That was a good trick," he said.
Arlo thought about it for a moment, and then he smiled, too. It was a good trick.
Then, Stanley stole one of the Sasquatch feet and they both burst out laughing.

Laughing made Arlo feel a lot better.
It made him realize that two wooden feet
were no reason to stop searching for something,
especially something as wonderful as Sasquatch.
Arlo and his father went back inside, took out
their map, and began to plan their next adventure.

That night, Arlo dreamed that he was
hiking through the woods with Sasquatch.
As they walked, Sasquatch told him
all the things about Sasquatches
that only Sasquatches know.